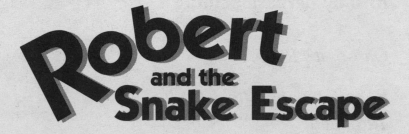

Robert
and the
Snake Escape

Also by Barbara Seuling

Oh No, It's Robert

Robert and the Attack of the Giant Tarantula

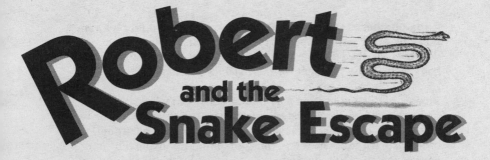

Robert
and the
Snake Escape

by Barbara Seuling
Illustrated by Paul Brewer

A
LITTLE APPLE
PAPERBACK

SCHOLASTIC INC.
New York Toronto London Auckland Sydney
Mexico City New Delhi Hong Kong Buenos Aires

No part of this publication may be reproduced in whole or in part, or stored in a retrieval system, or transmitted in any form or by any means, electronic, mechanical, photocopying, recording, or otherwise, without written permission of the publisher. For information regarding permission, write to Carus Publishing Company, 315 Fifth Street, Peru, Illinois 61354.

ISBN 0-439-23546-4

12 11 10 9 8 7 6 5   2 3 4 5 6/0

Printed in the U.S.A.
First Scholastic printing, October 2001

Contents

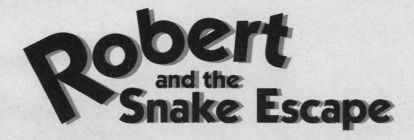

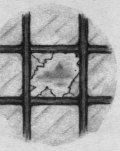

The Broken Window

"**C**ome on, Paul. Our line is moving!" Robert raced across the school yard. His friend Paul Felcher was right behind him.

"What's your rush?" asked Paul. "Sally won't go anywhere without you."

"I know," said Robert, "but she's been alone all weekend."

Sally was a two-foot-long ribbon snake. Mrs. Bernthal had bought Sally for the class at the beginning of the school year. Everyone in Robert's class knew he loved animals.

He even had a pet-sitting service of his own. So when Mrs. Bernthal needed a snake monitor, Robert was the class's first choice.

Robert fell in love with Sally right away. She was as green as the moss on the bottom of the terrarium in the Nature Corner. Robert loved the way Sally made a little *S* curve when he gently stroked her back.

Robert and Paul followed the rest of the class up the stairs to room 204. The door was locked, so Mrs. Bernthal opened it with her key. A blast of cold air came out of the room and hit them in the face.

"Oh, my," said Mrs. Bernthal. "What happened in here?" She went inside. The dinosaur skeleton was knocked over on its side. Water had soaked the diorama of a prehistoric jungle that Paul had finished just last week. Papers had blown off the bulletin board and were all over the floor.

"The window is broken," said Susanne Lee Rodgers, pointing. One pane in the middle window was broken and jagged. Cold air blew through it.

"That's funny. There's no broken glass on the floor. I'll ask Mr. Soler to fix it," said Mrs. Bernthal. Mr. Soler was the school custodian. She wrote a reminder on the blackboard: SEE CUSTODIAN.

The children rushed to the coat closet to put away their coats and jackets.

"Wait, children!" Mrs. Bernthal called after them. "Better keep your coats on. It's cold in here." Everyone hurried to their desks still wearing their outside clothes.

"Children," called Mrs. Bernthal, picking up a paper. "Let's get our classroom back in order. You may all help by picking up the papers that were blown around."

Vanessa Nicolini found a few drawings that were still in good shape. She tacked them back up on the bulletin board.

Paul picked up torn and dirty papers that had been walked on. He dropped them in the wastebasket.

While the other children cleaned up the papers, Robert made his way to the back of the room. That's where Sally lived in her glass tank.

He walked over to the tank and stared.
"Sally is gone!" he cried.

The Snake
Is Loose!

All the children stopped what they were doing.

"You mean, the snake is loose?" cried Matt Blakey.

"Aieee-eee!" screamed Melissa Thurm. She ran and hid in the coat closet. Mrs. Bernthal went after her to calm her down and convince her that Sally was not dangerous.

Robert remembered the day Mrs. Bernthal first brought Sally into class. Melissa had screamed, "Snakes are slimy and dirty!" Robert knew that wasn't true. Sally was smooth and clean.

Paul ran over to Robert. "How did Sally get loose?" he asked.

"The lid was off the tank," said Robert. He looked at the lid, which was on the table next to the tank. "I'm sure I put it back on before we went home on Friday."

"Maybe you forgot and thought you did," said Paul.

"Maybe," Robert said, scratching his head.

The other children crowded around Sally's empty tank. Robert looked under the sand and stones in the tank, just in case. Sally was not there.

Mrs. Bernthal came out of the coat closet with Melissa by the hand. "Class, I'm taking Melissa over to stay in Ms. Bright's room for a while. Look around the room for Sally. I'll be right back."

The children checked their desks, the
floor, and the supply cabinet. No Sally.
Robert and Paul searched the coat closet.
Still no Sally.

"Maybe she went out the broken window," said Susanne Lee.

Robert looked out the window down at the playground. They were on the second floor. He hoped Susanne Lee was wrong. But Susanne Lee Rodgers knew everything. She was almost never wrong.

"Maybe Sally went home because she hates school," said Lester Willis. Lester made corny jokes about everything.

A few minutes later, Mrs. Bernthal came back. It was clear the class had not found Sally.

"Thank you, class, for your help," she said, putting on her gloves. "Take your seats now. Robert, you may continue to look for Sally. I know if anyone can find her, you can."

"Can I help?" asked Paul.

"*May* I," said Mrs. Bernthal.

"May I help?"

"Yes, you may. I'll see about getting that window fixed."

Mrs. Bernthal had the class open their spelling books. Robert and Paul went back to the class library to decide what to do. Robert pulled out a book about snakes. He

turned to the chapter about eating habits. Paul looked over his shoulder. Robert read that snakes could live for a whole week without eating. He had fed Sally on Friday and now it was Monday.

"She's not going to starve for four more days," he whispered, closing the book. "But we've still got to find her. She must be scared."

"We'll find her," said Paul.

Robert wished he could believe him.

The Search
Continues

"Line up, class," said Mrs. Bernthal. "We'll find a warmer place to work until the window is fixed. Vanessa, will you please go to Ms. Bright's room and bring Melissa back?"

As the children lined up at the door, Mrs. Bernthal handed a note to Kevin Kransky. "Kevin, will you please take this down to Mr. Soler in the basement?"

The basement! Everyone looked at Kevin. Robert felt sorry for him. Nobody wanted to go to the basement. It was a scary place.

Kevin took the note bravely.

"Boys," said Mrs. Bernthal to Robert, Paul, and Kevin, "the rest of us will be in the auditorium, where it is warm. When you come back, please join us there."

"Yeah! We're getting out of here, just like Sally!" said Matt Blakey.

The class giggled as they followed Mrs. Bernthal down the hall. Robert heard Mrs. Bernthal's voice. "Remember, you are the best class in the whole world. I expect good behavior from you."

The first place Robert and Paul looked for Sally was outside, under the window of their classroom. Maybe Sally had slithered down the vines that clung to the building wall.

There was no sign of Sally anywhere.

"How do you think our window got broken?" asked Paul.

"I don't know. Someone could have thrown a rock."

"But then we would have found a rock in our classroom," said Paul.

"That's true," said Robert. "Hey! I just thought of something."

"What?"

"A show I saw on TV said that snakes are cold-blooded. That means they have to stay in warm places to heat their bodies."

"Hmm." Paul scratched his head. "Maybe Matt was right. Our class left our room because it was too cold. Maybe Sally did, too."

"She wouldn't go out the window," said Robert. "It's even colder out here than it was in the classroom."

"Yeah," said Paul. "It was cold and rainy over the weekend, too."

"We have to find her soon," said Robert. "She might die if she gets too cold."

"Sally is smart," said Paul. "Maybe she found a warm place."

"Yeah," said Robert. "So she must still be inside. Let's go back. Maybe we missed her."

Robert and Paul ran inside, heading for the stairway. They met Kevin coming up from the basement. He was panting.

"Hi, Kevin. Did you give the note to Mr. Soler?" asked Robert. He admired Kevin for going to the basement on his own.

"I left it on his desk," Kevin answered. "Mr. Soler wasn't there."

Robert could imagine Kevin dropping the note like a hot potato and running. Well, he would have done the same thing if he had to go to the basement.

16

Kevin headed for the auditorium, and Robert and Paul went upstairs. The door to room 204 was still open. They went in.

"Brrr!" said Paul.

"I wonder if Sally squeezed out under the door," said Robert.

Paul knelt down to examine the space under the door. "Sally couldn't fit under here," he said, getting up.

Robert scratched his head. "She didn't go outside, and she couldn't get out of the room. She's got to be here. In a warm place." He dragged a chair over to the coat closet.

"What are you doing?" asked Paul.

"I'm checking everything this time," Robert said. He climbed on the chair to look on the shelf above the coat hooks. There was a baseball cap, a notebook, and a brown paper bag with a stale cheese sandwich in it. There was a boot and a rolled-up poster. There was no snake.

Next he opened the supply cabinet. Together, he and Paul took out all the supplies. They wanted to be sure Sally wasn't hiding behind them. Then they put them all back again.

They felt behind all the books on the bookshelves. Sally wasn't there.

They looked behind the radiator. She wasn't there, either.

The clock on the wall showed a whole hour had gone by. They still had not found Sally. Then Robert turned over the wastebasket to empty it, just in case Sally was inside. Suddenly he noticed a torn piece of paper with a heel mark on it. Words were printed on it in black marker.

"Oh, no! Look at this!"

Paul came running. He read the note and gasped.

"Sally's been kidnapped!" he cried.

No Time
to Lose

"**W**ho is Dian?" asked Paul.

"I have no idea. And why would she kidnap Sally?" Robert tried not to panic.

"I don't know," said Paul.

They went over to Sally's tank.

"That explains why the lid is off the tank," said Robert. "I knew I didn't leave it off."

"Yeah," said Paul. "It was Dian."

"We'd better tell Mrs. Bernthal," said Robert.

They found her and their class in the auditorium.

They ran down the aisle. "We know what happened to Sally!" cried Robert, waving the torn piece of paper. Paul was right behind him.

"That's good, boys. Class, be quiet," called Mrs. Bernthal as the children started to buzz. She turned back to Robert and Paul. "Where did you find her?"

"No, we didn't find her. We—"

"No talking, Emily. Please do your math problems."

"We found a note—"

"Give me my book!" begged Melissa, who looked like she was about to cry. "Mrs. Bernthal, Matt took my book." Matt was balancing a book on his head.

"Matt, stop fooling around," said Mrs. Bernthal. "Class, I want you to behave like ladies and gentlemen."

She turned back to Robert and Paul. "I'm sorry. What were you saying?"

"We found a note," said Robert.

Tap, tap, tap.

Lester was up in front of the auditorium. He was tapping the podium with his pencil, pretending to be a conductor. Soon everyone was laughing and tapping their pencils.

"Very funny, Lester," said Mrs. Bernthal. "Sit down now. Class, when you finish your math, I'd like you to write an essay about why Lester makes you laugh."

Everyone groaned.

Mrs. Bernthal turned back to Robert and Paul. "Oh. Sorry. Where were we?"

"Is it okay if we keep looking for Sally?" asked Robert, dropping his jacket on an empty seat. Paul dropped his, too. Robert stuffed the note into his jeans pocket.

"I suppose so. Good luck, boys."

"She's too busy to talk right now," said Robert as he and Paul left the auditorium. "We have to figure it out ourselves. There's no time to lose. The kidnapper may not know that Sally could die if she doesn't stay warm."

They sat down in the stairway to think. "It had to be someone with a key to the classroom," said Paul. "The door was locked when we came in this morning, remember?"

"Mrs. Bernthal has the key," said Robert.

"But Mrs. Bernthal wouldn't take Sally. She bought her for us," said Paul. "Besides, her name isn't Dian. It's Janet. I saw it on a paper once."

"Dian could be a fake name. The kidnapper may be using it to cover up her real name." Robert drummed his fingers on the step. "Who else has a key to our classroom?"

"What about Mike, the janitor?" said Paul. "He cleans our room when we're not there. He must have a key."

"Let's go find him. We'll start on the top floor." They flew up the stairs to find Mike.

The Suspects

Robert and Paul checked the hall and every closet and bathroom on the fourth floor. It was a little tricky going into the girls' bathroom. First they knocked. When there was no answer, Robert went in while Paul waited outside. Paul promised to pound on the door if any girl came by.

They finished the fourth floor and were halfway through the third floor when they found Mike fixing a sink in the boys' bathroom.

"Hi, Mike," said Robert.

Mike looked up. "Hi. What brings you guys up here?" Mike's muscles bulged under his shirt. He held a huge wrench in his hand.

"Um . . . did you see a snake?" asked Paul.

"A snake!" said Mike. He got up so fast he nearly hit his head on the sink.

"No. Not here," said Robert. "Our snake is missing—from room 204."

"I sure don't have it," said Mike. "I hate snakes." He shivered and went back to work under the sink.

Paul turned to leave with Robert right behind him. Then he stopped. "Mike, do you know anyone around here named Dian?"

"No," said Mike. He peered over a pipe. "Why?"

"We think that's who has our snake," said Robert.

"I don't know any Dian," said Mike. "And I didn't see your snake. But I did see the broken window in your room this morning. I reported it to Mr. Soler. It's next on my list of things to do today. There'd better not be any snake around when I go in there!"

"Who else besides you has a key to our room?" asked Paul.

"Mr. Soler," Mike said. "He has all the keys to the building."

Robert grabbed Paul by the sleeve. "Thanks, Mike!" He pulled Paul out of the bathroom into the hall. "Come on! We have to find Mr. Soler!"

"Wait a minute," said Paul, stopping short.

Robert stopped, too. "What?"

"Mr. Soler!" said Paul. "His office is in the basement!"

Robert felt a cold shiver. In first and second grade, Paul and Robert imagined that a monster made the terrible noises they sometimes heard coming from the basement. Now that they were in third grade, they were too old to believe in monsters.

Still, they thought terrible things happened down there.

The boiler room was in the basement. What was boiled in it? It sounded like a witch's cauldron, hissing and bubbling and brewing.

Robert knew he had to be brave. Kevin had gone down there, and nothing had happened to him. Besides, Mrs. Bernthal was counting on him.

"You don't have to go," he told Paul. "But I have to. I'm the snake monitor."

Paul swallowed hard. "I'm going with you," he said.

Together, they went down the stairs to the basement. They didn't run this time. They walked down slowly, as quietly as they could.

The Basement

"This is creepy," whispered Paul.

"It's just the basement," said Robert.

"I know. But it's more like Dracula's castle."

Robert knew what Paul meant. The basement smelled like old paint. The walls were gray cinder blocks and the floor was made of concrete. There were pipes on the walls and ceiling. It didn't look anything like the rest of the school, which was bright and cheerful.

In the background, they heard hissing and rumbling. "The monster!" Paul said, the way he had done when they were in second grade.

"Yeah, right," said Robert, looking around nervously. "It's a good thing we know better."

They found a door marked D. SOLER, CUSTODIAN. Robert pointed to the D. "The D could be for Dian," he whispered.

"Or Dracula," said Paul.

Robert's hands were shaking, but he knocked on the door.

"Come in," answered a deep voice.

Robert opened the door. Like a huge beast, the pipes continued to bang and hiss. Robert felt like Dorothy in *The Wizard of Oz.* When she and her friends the Tin Man, the Lion, and the Scarecrow entered the hall of the great wizard, there was a roaring and a hissing, too.

Mr. Soler didn't look anything like a wizard. He was sitting at a desk. The light

from his desk lamp made his glasses shiny.
Robert couldn't see his eyes.

"Hello, boys," said Mr. Soler. He
grinned, showing his teeth. "Come on in.
I've been expecting you."

34

Safe and Sound

Robert's hands felt clammy. His mouth went dry. "You . . . you have?" he asked.

"Yes," said Mr. Soler, getting up. "Come with me."

Robert's knees were shaking. He and Paul followed Mr. Soler through a door to a big dark room. The noise was deafening. A monster machine rumbled and clanked and hissed. "That's the boiler," Mr. Soler shouted over the noise. "That's what heats the whole school."

The room was toasty warm. Mr. Soler led them to a corner next to the boiler. There, on a shelf, in a shoe box with a piece of screen over it, was Sally.

"Sally!" cried Robert. He ran over to the box and picked her up. As he stroked her smooth body, Sally wiggled into a little *S* curve.

"You took our snake?" asked Paul.

"Yes, I did," said Mr. Soler.

"Why?" asked Robert.

"Well, Mike told me this morning there was a broken window in your room. I went up to inspect it. The window was broken, all right. I found glass on the floor, and a rock. Someone must have thrown it. We had some pretty bad weather over the weekend, so it was cold in there."

Robert remembered the branches of the apple tree in his yard banging into his window at night and rain drumming on the roof.

"I figured I'd better bring your snake down here until the window was fixed," Mr. Soler continued. "I used to catch snakes when I was a boy, in Puerto Rico. Snakes don't like the cold. I put her in my pocket and took her to the nice warm boiler room. She didn't seem to mind." He looked over his glasses. "Didn't you see my note? I taped it on the snake's tank."

"You mean this?" Robert pulled the torn paper out of his pocket and handed it to Mr. Soler. "We thought it was from someone named Dian."

"Hmmm," said Mr. Soler, looking at the paper. "This is only part of the note I left. What happened to it?"

"The wind must have blown it off the tank," said Paul, figuring it out. "Then it landed on the floor, and someone walked on it."

Mr. Soler pulled a folded piece of paper

from his pocket. He smoothed it out, blank side up, and wrote something. He showed it to Robert and Paul. "This is what I wrote," he said.

The paper read:

I'VE GOT YOUR SNAKE

SEE CUSTODIAN

"Oh, no! Custo-DIAN." Robert rolled his eyes at Paul.

Mr. Soler laughed. "Anyway, your snake is safe, but I'm sure she would like to come back to your classroom. We'd better get your window fixed so you can take her home."

"Thanks for keeping Sally warm," said Robert, picking up the shoe box.

"Yeah," said Paul. "You probably saved her life."

"What does the D in your name stand for?" asked Robert.

"Danielo," said Mr. Soler. "Why?"

"We just wondered." Robert smiled at Paul as they left the boiler room with the shoe box.

Bringing Sally Home

Robert and Paul knew not to run with Sally in the shoe box, but they walked as fast as they could.

Paul pulled open the auditorium door. "We found her!" he shouted. The class turned around to see them come in.

Mrs. Bernthal smiled. "You boys are terrific," she said. "Come and tell us how you did it. Where was she?"

"In the basement," said Robert. Several children gasped.

41

"We have a few minutes before the lunch bell rings," said Mrs. Bernthal. "Why don't you come up and tell us about it."

Robert and Paul went to the front of the auditorium. Robert began. He talked about how Sally could have died if she got too cold.

Paul filled in some places. He made the boiler room sound like Dracula's castle. Melissa covered her ears.

When they were finished, the class applauded, except for Melissa. Lester and Matt both whistled.

Everyone had questions. They all wanted to see Sally up close. Mrs. Bernthal let the children come up and see Sally. She didn't even tell them they had to finish their math work first.

A knock at the back of the auditorium stopped their chatter. Mike stood in the doorway.

"Hello, Mike," Mrs. Bernthal said. "Did you want to see me?"

"Your window will be fixed when you come back from lunch," he said. "I'm working on it right now."

"Thanks, Mike." Mrs. Bernthal turned to the class. "I think this day deserves something special," she said.

"A party?" said Vanessa.

"Even better. This afternoon, I'm going to read you a story."

"What kind of story?" asked Lester.

"A story about a snake," said Mrs. Bernthal.

Melissa squealed.

"It's called 'Rikki-Tikki-Tavi,'" said Mrs. Bernthal. "It was written by a man named Rudyard Kipling. I think you will enjoy it. Even you, Melissa," she said, smiling at Melissa.

"No more math?" asked Matt Blakey.

"No," said Mrs. Bernthal, grinning. "No more math. Come, children. Get your things together and line up."

Robert and Paul walked downstairs to the cafeteria. Mrs. Bernthal said it was okay to take Sally with them as long as she stayed in her box. Room 204 would be a lot warmer after lunch.

"You know, I'm going to get a lamp for Sally's tank," said Robert. "Then she'll always be warm, no matter what."

"I think I'm going to paint Sally's name on her tank in fancy letters," said Paul.

Robert peeked over the shoulder of the boy in front of him in the cafeteria line. Hot dogs! Robert thought this day was really working out fine. He stroked Sally gently and smiled as she made her little *S* curve.

46

BARBARA SEULING is a well-known author of fiction and nonfiction books for children, including several books about Robert. She divides her time between New York City and Vermont.

PAUL BREWER likes to draw gross, silly situations, which is why he enjoys working on books about Robert so much. He lives in San Diego, California, with his wife and two daughters.